By ROMEO MULLER

Illustrations by
Fred Wolf and Chuck Swenson
Based on the TV Special

PUFF THE MAGIC DRAGON
is an original publication of Avon Books.
This work has never before appeared in book form.

"Puff (The Magic Dragon)" Words by Peter Yarrow and Leonard Lipton.

"The Boat Song" Words and Music by Peter Yarrow.

"Weave Me The Sunshine" Words and Music by Peter Yarrow.

Illustrations by Fred Wolf and Chuck Swenson
based on the TV special

AVON BOOKS
A division of
The Hearst Corporation
959 Eighth Avenue
New York, New York 10019

Published by arrangement with The My Company.
Library of Congress Catalog Card Number: 79-51610
ISBN: 0-380-45807-1

First Camelot Printing, September, 1979

Printed in the U.S.A.

Book design by Joan Walton

Dedicated to
Peter, Paul, and Mary

CONTENTS

One. "Jackie Draper, Meet Jackie Paper"
· 7 ·

Two. Very Long John
· 19 ·

Three. The Sea of the Starless Skies
· 30 ·

Four. Honah Lee
· 35 ·

Five. Home at Last
· 49 ·

Songs

The Boat Song
· 54 ·

Weave Me the Sunshine
· 58 ·

CHAPTER ONE

"Jackie Draper, Meet Jackie Paper"

Once, quite by chance, there was an extraordinary old universe. And it was filled with matter and magnificence; with worlds and wonder; with moons and magic. And moving through this universe was a familiar old world of cities and streets; of tree and cars. There, in an ordinary house, on an ordinary chair, was a boy. And in the boy's head was locked an untold story which was as extraordinary as anything that old universe had ever seen or heard.

The boy sat quietly, surrounded by his mother, his father, and three learned doctors.

The doctors turned to the boy's parents grimly, and the tallest of them spoke. "We have concluded our consultation and find that your son will not, nor cannot, speak, communicate, nor relate in any way to the world around him."

"But doctors, we know that," said the father sadly. "He hasn't said a word for such a long time."

"Can't you give us some hope that he will someday be able to speak again?" pleaded the little boy's mother.

The tall doctor cut her off with a wave of his hand. "Alas, the case is hopeless."

The mother and father looked at each other sorrowfully, then followed the doctors out of the room, closing the door softly behind them.

The boy's name was Jackie Draper. He was only eight years old, but magnificent things were about to happen to him.

Puff the magic dragon
Lived by the sea
And frolicked in the autumn mist
In a land called Honah Lee.

Jackie Draper seemed to hear the song deep inside his heart. And at that very moment, a large face passed by outside his window. It was all green, with dark green eyebrows, strands of even greener hair, and friendly green chin whiskers down below. The face was there for just an instant, and then was gone.

Suddenly it popped back into view, smiled, and looked into the room. "I beg your pardon," said Puff, trying to start a proper conversation. "Could you tell me if you just saw a dragon pass by?"

Jackie sat still and silent.

"I could swear I saw one. Most unusual nowadays," continued Puff, searching Jackie's room with his eyes. He spied his own reflection in the mirror above Jackie's bureau. "Ah, I did see one! Me!"

The boy did not reply, but merely blinked his sad little eyes.

"May I consider that blink an invitation?" chuckled Puff. Without waiting for a reply, he began to climb in through the window, which was really much too small to admit a full-grown dragon. "I shall have to make myself smaller to fit. No trouble. Just magic."

There was a tinkling, like the sound of silver bells, and in an instant Puff was the size of a large, friendly dog. He easily climbed into the room, put down his battered old satchel, and smiled at the boy. "I've come to help you, Jackie. To help you help yourself."

Jackie Draper managed to make a tiny, halfhearted smile.

Puff opened up his satchel. Magical sparkles flew out like giddy June bugs in July. He searched for something in his bag, tossing out various objects that were common to him but totally wondrous to Jackie. There was the famous glass slipper, Alice's mushroom, Peter's shadow, gold spun from straw, and a yellow brick or two. Finally he found a large piece of construction paper, a crayon, and a pair of scissors.

Going about his magic business in a way both magical and businesslike, he tacked the construction paper to the wall. Then, using the crayon, which could color every hue and shade of the rainbow, he began to draw a picture of Jackie Draper. As he worked, he chattered cheerfully.

"I'm one of the few dragons ever to have a song of my own. That is because instead of destroying things, I try to muddle through. Ah, splendid likeness of you, Jackie, if I do say so myself."

Using the scissors he snipped the crayon drawing of Jackie Draper free from the rest of

the construction paper and brought it over to the boy.

"Jackie Draper, this is Jackie Paper," said Puff, introducing the real boy to the cutout. "Now, Jackie Draper, I am going to borrow the 'living-thing' from inside you and place it inside Jackie Paper."

The little smile froze on the boy's lips, and Puff realized he was frightened.

"You wonder what a 'living-thing' is?" asked Puff quietly. "Let me explain. It is that which causes you to laugh and cry, to hurt and to care. It is that which makes apples crunchy and tells your nose to tingle on a crystal winter's morning." Then he leaned down and whispered gently. "It's kept in your left ear, you know."

He puffed some brightly colored dragon smoke into Jackie's right ear. The smoke billowed out of the boy's left ear, carrying with it the shadowy outline of a small child. Puff took the fragile "living-thing" by the hand and rushed it over to Jackie Paper, chattering, "Quick! Mustn't catch cold!"

With a gentle shove he pushed it into Jackie Paper. The cutout child suddenly took on rounded form and came to life. He blinked his eyes, took a breath, and spoke.

"Am I all better?" asked Jackie Paper.

Puff chuckled playfully. "Well, we'll see. To be truly better you must make a journey with me. Impossible for Jackie Draper. But Jackie *Paper*—he can go anywhere, so long as it is magic. Come along, now." He held out his paw.

Jackie pulled back, worried. "But where are we going, Puff?"

"Ha-ha-ha! Good question, Jackie! We are going to Honah Lee."

"What's Honah Lee?" asked Jackie.

"My kingdom by the sea. Well, it's not exactly **A KINGDOM**," he boomed in a great big voice. "It's more like *a kingdom*," he squeaked in a tiny baby voice. "A few acres and independence. But it *is* rather magical. Let me show you."

He blew a colored ring of dragon smoke, which Jackie looked through, as one might look through an enchanted porthole.

Jackie gasped with wonder. For stretching out in front of him was an incredible island of mountains and coral and magic. There were fat, hearty trees with friendly faces, whose leaves of russet and gold shaded great flocks of wild flowers with happy faces. A warm, sandy beach of pure white sloped down and embraced a calm and crystal sea of the purest blue. Squatting on the horizon was a smiling sun casting its golden warmth onto a population of birds, butterflies, and animals, both mundane and mythological. Jackie recognized a pink rabbit and a unicorn colt. Through the center drifted a gentle stream from which sweet mists rose and hung lazily on the glistening afternoon. It was a wonderful place, a land of peace and joy.

"Oh, Puff. It's beautiful. Is it far away?"

"As far as your fondest hope. And, hopefully, as near as your sweetest dream." He took Jackie by the hand. "Come along. We'll build a boat."

Jackie pulled back. "I'm afraid!"

Puff smiled. "Well, isn't everybody?" He knelt down and spoke to the paper child gently. "Aw, Jackie, that's why I want you to visit Honah Lee. The climate there causes fear to shrivel up and makes it as useless as last year's calendar."

"But Puff, we've got to *get* there first. And I'm afraid of the sea."

Puff looked at Jackie, concerned. Then he walked over to the window and pulled down the shade. He held out his crayon to the boy and said, "I want you to draw a picture of the sea on this window shade."

"Okay," said Jackie, "but I warn you, it's going to be scary!" He began to draw a terrifying picture of the sea. It was more like a nightmare than a drawing. There were great waves and storms and lightning flashes and shipwrecks. There were sharks and an octopus, and, worst of all, a terrible giant pirate!

"No wonder you are frightened," said Puff. "I suppose the sea *can* be that way. But if you'll just look through my dragon smoke, I'll show you how it *might* be." And he puffed another colorful ring, which floated up to Jackie's window-shade drawing and changed it into a lovely calm blue sea, sparkling gloriously in the sun.

Jackie came over to the dragon, hesitated for an instant, then impulsively embraced him. "I like you, Puff!" he said. "Let's build a boat!"

"With what?" asked the dragon.

"I've got stuff! All kinds of stuff!" He rushed over to his toy box and dumped its contents on the floor.

Little Jackie Paper
Loved that rascal, Puff,
And brought him strings and sealing wax
And other fancy stuff.

Jackie got a great idea. He cried out, "Hey! We can use my bed as the hull!"

"MAGNIFICENT!" roared Puff. "We'll cross the ocean on a magic boat," he sang.

And Jackie sang, "We'll make the main-mast out of my bedpost! Let's make the rudder out of my guitar!"

"And sail across the water!" they both sang.

In no more time than it took to sing the words, they had built themselves the finest little boat they could wish for. They hopped aboard and sailed off into the beautiful sea painted on the window shade. They were on their way to Honah Lee at last!

CHAPTER TWO

Very Long John

Together they would travel
On a boat with billowed sail,
Jackie kept a lookout perched
On Puff's gigantic tail.

It really *was* a gigantic tail again. For once Puff left the confines of Jackie's bedroom, he returned to full dragon size. Jackie, riding tall in the tail, scanned the horizon and finally spotted another ship.

"AHOY!" he shouted to the H.M.S.

Bicycle, which was manned by a crew of living playing cards.

"AHOY!" they shouted back, and all the picture cards bowed down.

Noble kings and princes
Would bow whene'er they came,
Pirate ships would low'r their flag
When Puff roared out his name.

"Pirates?" cried Jackie, terrified once more. He slid down Puff's tail and landed in the dragon's arms. "I don't want to see any pirates! Puff, I'm afraid. Take me home."

Puff looked quite surprised. "Jackie, didn't you know? Once you set out for Honah Lee, there is no turning back. To find your way home, you must first find Honah Lee."

Suddenly there was a thundering sound, as if all the storms in creation had combined into one. A huge wave billowed under the boat, lifting it higher and higher. Then the wave seemed to turn into a great hand, the smallest finger of which was bigger than Jackie. The thunder turned into an earsplitting peal of laughter, which rolled out of a gigantic mouth at the bottom of an enormous, ugly face that leered down at them with a malicious fury.

Jackie screamed, for he recognized the great giant pirate in his nightmare window-shade drawing.

"GOTCHA!" roared the pirate. "YOU'LL NEVER GET AWAY!" He was as tall as a sky-scraper and as strong as a barrel of earth-quakes, and he sloshed through the raging sea as if it were a schoolyard puddle.

"Now *that* is a pirate!" said Puff.

"I'M LONG JOHN! V-E-R-Y LONG

BLACK AND BLUEBEARD KIDD," he chanted. "I'M BIGGER THAN BIG, AND HERE I REIGN. I'M THE MAIN SPANISH PIRATE OF THE SPANISH MAIN!"

"He certainly *is* very long," said Puff.

"SILENCE!" roared Very Long John as he brought the boat to an eerie, desolate island with a tall, angry-looking volcano in the center, surrounded by many smaller mountains and cliffs. One of the cliffs had a large skull and crossbones painted on the side. The pirate placed the boat down and, glowering at Puff and Jackie, burst into thunderclaps of laughter once more.

The awful sound hurled Jackie to the deck. He picked himself up and hid behind the dragon. "What are you going to do with us?" he shouted.

"HAVE NO FEAR. I WILL THINK OF SOMETHING—*TERRIBLE*!" roared the pirate.

Jackie went tumbling again. He got to his feet and ran to the magic dragon. "What do we do now, Puff?"

Puff smiled calmly. "He said it, Jackie. Have no fear."

"I'm scared to have no fear."

"Jackie, the first step in not being afraid is to see things as they really are. Watch!" He blew a magic ring of dragon smoke, which floated between Jackie and Very Long. The boy looked through the ring, and instead of a giant pirate, he saw a huge, friendly baker with a white apron and chef's hat.

"Puff, you mean underneath all that pirate stuff, Very Long John Black and Bluebeard Kidd is just a baker at heart?"

The dragon sucked back the smoke as if

it were a strand of spaghetti, nodded yes, and said, "Take care of him, Jackie. Use your wits. You can do it."

Jackie turned and walked across the deck until he faced the huge pirate, alone.

Very Long laughed, picked the boy up with one hand, dropped him, then caught him with the other. He roared, "WELL, LITTLE BOY, WHAT ARE YOUR LAST WORDS?"

Jackie must have had a very brave thought, for instead of answering the pirate with words, he sang, "Can you bake a cherry pie, Very Long, Very Long? Can you bake a cherry pie, Very Long John?"

The huge pirate was stunned for a moment. Then he rose to the challenge and sang back at Jackie, "I CAN BAKE A CHERRY PIE—QUICK AS A BAT CAN WINK ITS EYE! PUMPKIN, PEACH, AND A HALF A DOZEN OTHERS!"

Somehow Jackie sensed he had the upper hand. He relaxed a bit, and, leaning against the pirate's thumb, he said, "I don't believe you. You're a pretty good pirate. But a baker? Never!"

Furious, Very Long tightened his hand about Jackie and roared again. Jackie wondered if he had gone too far with the big fellow.

"I WILL DESTROY YOU!" roared the pirate. "BUT FIRST I WILL MAKE YOU EAT YOUR WORDS!"

He dropped Jackie down on the deck, turned, dashed back to the volcano at the center of the island, opened a door in the crater, and proceeded to bake a great stack of steaming pies. Presently, he came back and placed the pies down on the deck next to Jackie and Puff. "EAT!" he commanded.

And eat they did, all night long and well into the following day. Finally, when the last pie pan had been scraped clean, Puff looked up and said, "I adore eating my words, but your pies are ever so much better."

"Best pies I ever tasted in my whole mouth," agreed Jackie.

Very Long looked down at them and giggled with delight. "Really? I have never been so happy!" And then he began to cry great tears of joy, which poured down on Jackie and Puff like rain. Puff took out his

umbrella.

"Oh, if only I could be a friendly giant baker instead of an evil giant pirate. But no! My father was an evil giant pirate. All my family have been evil giant pirates! For generations!"

"But you can always change," said Jackie. "Everybody can change. Can't they, Puff?"

"So I'm given to understand," said Puff, winking at Jackie.

Jackie looked up at Very Long again. "Just make up your mind and do it! And you're so big you've just *got* to have lots of mind to make up!"

The next day, Very Long John, dressed in his baker's suit, gently placed the boat into the water and, with a hearty breath from his great lungs, sent it sailing toward Honah Lee once more. He waved farewell to his friends and cried out joyfully, "I am a new man! No! I am an old man with a new heart! Thank you both! And Godspeed."

Soon Very Long and his island were just a speck on the horizon to Jackie and Puff. They could hear him shouting a promise in the distance: "I'll send you a fruitcake next Christmas."

CHAPTER THREE

The Sea of the Starless Skies

The next few days passed blissfully, all blue skies and whitecapped waves, and the nights dazzled with starlight. But then, dark gray clouds appeared on the horizon and soon filled the sky with their cold and melancholy gloom. Puff and Jackie had to huddle together for warmth.

"Where are we now, Puff?"

The dragon was grim. "We've reached the Sea of the Starless Skies, Jackie."

The clouds formed themselves into mean

and ugly faces. Their cheeks puffed out, and they blew angry winds. Jackie felt a dark unfriendliness all about him. He turned to Puff. "I hate this old Sea of the Starless Skies," he said.

"It's not the sea's fault," said Puff. "It's the clouds. The clouds are jealous of the stars. You see, the stars can fly a thousand, thousand times higher than those clouds can even imagine. And so, like all small spirited, stupid things, they believe that they can deny beauty by hiding it."

"Puff! Look!" Jackie pointed up to the sky. A flickering glow was tumbling down through the cloud heads. It was a falling star, no bigger than a firefly. It landed with a gentle *poof*! on the deck. Jackie looked down at it. "Aw, the poor little thing."

The great cloud heads began to laugh. "Listen to them," said Puff. "They're always happy when a star dies."

"But she's not dead, Puff. Listen!"

The star made tiny, desperate sounds.

Jackie turned to Puff. "She wants to talk, but can't. Gee, I know just how she feels. We've got to save her!"

"To do that, we'd have to hang her back onto her orbit, Jackie. How would we get up there?"

"Well, we'll just make the boat fly! Use your magic, Puff. Paint some wings!"

"Why don't I paint some wings?" said Puff, as if he'd just thought of it. He reached into his satchel and brought out a paint-brush. He jumped off the boat and proceeded to paint two giant butterfly wings on thin air! Attaching them to the boat, he hopped back aboard and commanded the craft to fly.

The great wings began to flap gracefully, and the boat moved forward. It rose a few feet above the water, then came back down with a clumsy *splat!*

"Too heavy!" shouted Puff. "We shall have to unload some ballast. Me!" He dived into the water. "Take her up, Jackie!"

"Alone? I don't know how! I'm afraid!"

"Jackie! Believe in yourself. Have the courage to try. That's the second step to not being afraid. You may fail, but at least you'll have made the effort."

Jackie looked at the star on the deck, growing weaker and dimmer. He knew what

he had to do. "I'll try, Puff," he said.

The great wings began to flap. The boat lifted up and suddenly soared heavenward. With Jackie alone at the helm, the boat with butterfly wings made its way up through the cloud heads, who, furious now, blew angry winds and caused it to twist and toss dangerously.

But Jackie grasped the guitar rudder firmly, and suddenly the boat burst through the ceiling of clouds into a magnificent starry sky of diamonds twinkling in the blackness.

"We did it!" Jackie cried. Then he reached down, picked up the tiny star, and tossed her away into her distant orbit.

As she sailed off, her light glowed more brightly. Jackie heard a small voice calling back, "Thank you-ooo . . ."

And she was one of the millions again.

CHAPTER FOUR

Honah Lee

The next day, back on the high seas, Puff presented Jackie with a gold medal on a purple ribbon. "For bravery above and beyond the call of dragons," he said quite officially.

"I was brave?" asked Jackie. "I took another step?"

Puff was about to answer, when suddenly the boat hit solid land with a sickening crunch, sending them both sprawling. They had been so busy with the medal ceremony that they had failed to notice the rock-strewn island looming up ahead of them.

"LAND HO!" shouted Jackie as he picked himself up.

"So it would seem," agreed Puff, looking about. "But . . . but . . . where *are* we?"

Oh, it was a grim and dreary sight: a dank gray place, seen through a sheet of icy rain, all wet and clammy and most unpleasant.

Puff gasped. "It can't be!"

"You recognize this place, Puff?"

The dragon nodded yes, then cried, "It's . . . it's . . . Honah Lee!"

A chill went through Jackie. "Honah Lee? But what happened to it?"

"Something terrible, Jackie, while I was gone."

Jackie pointed to the beach. "Come on, let's take a look around."

Puff pulled back. "No, I'm afraid!" And he flopped down like a big, frightened puppy dog.

Jackie was astounded. *"You,* Puff? Afraid?"

"Uh-huh," nodded Puff.

"Just like *I* was before you came?"

"Uh-huh."

"Well, it's my turn to help now. Come on!" He held out his hand. Puff took it tentatively, and the two of them made their way up onto the rocky beach.

Presently they came upon a group of signs poking up from behind a large, ugly boulder. Puff read them aloud:

"BOW DOWN LOW!"
"GET ON YOUR KNEES-ES!"
"YOU ARE NOW ON THE ISLE"
"OF THE LIVING SNEEZES!"

Some more signs popped up, and Jackie read them:

"THIS MEANS YOU!"
"KA-CHOO!"
"YOU TOO!"

"What on earth is a living sneeze?" asked Puff.

As if to answer him, a strange creature leaped out from behind the rock. It was mostly an enormous red nose, with a small mouth under it, and little, bleary eyes above. "KAAAA-CHOOO!" it explained.

YOU ARE NOW ON THE ISLE
THIS MEANS YOU!

OF THE LIVING SNEEZES!
GET ON YOUR
YOU TOO!

Jackie ran up to it. "Are you a living sneeze, sir?" he asked politely.

"What do I look like, a hiccup?" said the sneeze nastily. "KA-CHOOOO!" it added.

Then several dozen other sneezes poked their noses over the rocks. "KA-CHOO! KA-CHOO! KA-CHOO! KA-CHOO!" they agreed.

Jackie turned to Puff. "Don't worry, Puff! I'll take care of this." And he walked up to the largest of the sneezes.

"Do you realize you are trespassing?" he asked.

"So what?! KA-CHOO!" sneered the sneeze.

"I'm sure Puff wouldn't mind," said Jackie. "He shares everything. But why do you ruin things?"

"Because we're uncomfortable! KA-CHOOOOO!" he explained.

And the other sneezes all nodded their noses. "Unnnnn-comfortable! KA-CHOO! KA-CHOO! KA-CHOO!" they repeated.

"But why are you uncomfortable?" asked Jackie.

"Wouldn't *you* be uncomfortable," said

the large sneeze, "If you were nothing but a nose, all stopped up and red and sore? KA-CHOO!" he argued.

Jackie understood his argument. He dashed back to his friend. "Puff! They are what they are because they feel so awful! Use your magic to make them better!"

Puff sighed. "Honah Lee is my magic. And if *it* is spoiled, so are my magic powers."

Jackie had never seen his friend so unhappy. At that moment, all the sneezes exploded into a symphony of "KA-CHOOS," and Puff looked more distressed than ever. He had never intended to bring Jackie into a situation such as this.

"Jackie, you must go home. You've completed your quest and don't seem frightened anymore."

"I wouldn't leave you, Puff."

Puff realized that in order to make Jackie leave he would have to pretend to be angry. He frowned and snapped, "I have all I can do to put up with the sneezes. You'd be just a bother to me. I want you to take the boat and go!"

Jackie felt crushed. Still, an order was an order. "Yessir, if you say so, Puff."

He turned and walked off. In a few moments he was back in the boat, sailing away from the terrible sneezy place Honah Lee had become.

Sadly, Puff watched Jackie go. Then he turned and walked along the barren beach to his cave. He had never felt so alone in his life.

The sneezes all slid down behind their slimy rocks and went to sleep. The cold rain continued to fall.

A dragon lives forever
But not so little boys,
Painted wings and giant rings
Make way for other toys.
One gray night it happened,
Jackie Paper came no more
And Puff that mighty dragon,
He ceased his fearless roar.

His head was bent in sorrow,
Green scales fell like rain,
Puff no longer went to play

Along the cherry lane.
Without his life-long friend,
Puff could not be brave
So Puff that mighty dragon,
Sadly slipped into his cave.

Puff lost track of the many days and nights he spent in that cave. He thought perhaps he would never come out again. Never! As a matter of fact, he was thinking this thought for the thousandth time when he heard a voice, far off in the distance.

"Puff! Puff! It's me! I'm back!"

The dragon lifted his great head and poked it out of the cave. "Could it be Jackie?" he wondered.

It certainly was! His little friend came sliding up to the cave as if he were a baseball player and Puff were home plate!

"What are you doing here?" cried Puff happily.

"Aw, Puff, you didn't think I'd leave you for good, did you? I went to get help. We'll fix those sneezes, Puff. Look who I brought!"

Puff looked up. Way up. Towering over the island was Very Long John, dressed in his

chef's suit. He carried a big pot of soup in one hand and a gigantic spoon in the other.

Jackie cried out, "Very Long, do your stuff!"

All this commotion awakened the sneezes. They poked their noses out from behind the rocks and watched as Very Long dipped the spoon into the pot and began to sprinkle its contents down onto them.

"NOSES DRIBBLE—NOSES DROOP!" he chanted. "WHAT YOU NEED IS MY CHICKEN SOUP!"

"Chicken soup?" said Puff, amazed.

"Best cure in the whole world for sneezes," said Jackie.

By now the chicken soup was pouring down all over the place, drenching the sneezes. At first they seemed frightened. But in a few seconds their little mouths turned upward in grins, and they began to chortle with delight.

"It's like rain!"

"But beautiful!"

"And all nummy, nummy, nummy!"

Soon, a large lake of soup had formed. The sneezes jumped in, floated on their

backs, splashed, and dunked each other playfully. Indeed, this was the most glorious moment of their sad, sniffling lives.

Before long, all their noses had become normal-sized, the soreness was gone, and the word "KA-CHOO!" was dropped from their vocabulary.

Jackie walked up to them, put his fingers in his mouth, and gave a sharp whistle to get their attention. "Okay, neighbors," he shouted, "now that you are all cured, let's fix up Honah Lee the way it used to be!" And because sometimes a song is more inspiring than mere words, he began to sing, "Weave, weave, weave me the sunshine out of the falling rain. Weave me the hope of a new tomorrow, and fill my cup again!"

Soon everybody began to sing. And the glorious song kept tempo with their work. And as they all worked and sang together, the color and beauty came back to Honah Lee. It was alive again, just as it had been before.

And finally, wonder of wonders, the little star, whom Jackie had saved, came soaring out of the skies like a fairy comet, the magic of her cosmic tail mingling with the falling rain and actually weaving it into sunshine.

Jackie closed his eyes for a second, and when he opened them again, he was back in his room at home.

CHAPTER FIVE

Home at Last

Jackie Paper looked about, mystified. Puff was there. And the real boy, Jackie Draper, still sat silently on his chair. The window shade was up, and the beautiful crayon sea was gone.

"Puff, why are we back in my room?"

"Because it is time for you to return. And time is stronger than magic."

"But Puff . . ."

Puff explained. "As I promised, you helped yourself. And in helping yourself, Jackie, you helped me. And now it is time to be truly brave. To face growing up. To be Jackie Draper again. And, eventually, to go beyond childish fancies, such as dragons, and not need them anymore." His eyes twinkled for just an instant. "Unless absolutely necessary," he added.

"No, Puff . . ."

"Come along, now," said Puff, as he reached toward Jackie Paper and plucked the "living-thing" free. The boy became a flat, cutout crayon drawing once more, and fluttered to the floor.

The dragon led the "living-thing" back to Jackie Draper and tucked it carefully back into the boy's left ear.

"It's all up to you, dear friend," he whispered. "Good-bye, Jackie."

He walked briskly to the window. He turned and looked back at Jackie with wonderment.

"Chicken soup?" he chuckled, as if he still couldn't believe it. Then he climbed out the window and was gone.

The little boy, Jackie Draper, who had sat silently all these years, suddenly opened his eyes. There was so much feeling inside him

now, so much he needed to say. Words seemed to dance up from his heart, then got lost on his tongue.

Making a great effort, he managed to get up from his chair. He started across the room —slowly at first, then more rapidly. He stumbled to the window and clung to the sill. Puff was going! Would he never see his best friend again? He had to speak. He *had* to!

He opened his mouth. . . .

And suddenly the words came—part crying, part pleading, part saying farewell:

"PUFF! PUFF!"

The door to the room flew open, and Jackie's parents rushed in, amazed at what they were seeing and hearing.

"JACKIE! JACKIE!" they both cried.

Jackie turned to them. And more words came:

"Mom? Dad?"

"He's talking!" said Mr. Draper.

"Oh, my son!" said Mrs. Draper.

Laughing and weeping, both ran to him and held him close to their hearts. It was a magic moment, too precious ever to forget.

For a dragon had helped make a miracle, and Jackie Draper was home at last.

SONGS

The Boat Song

Words and music by Peter Yarrow

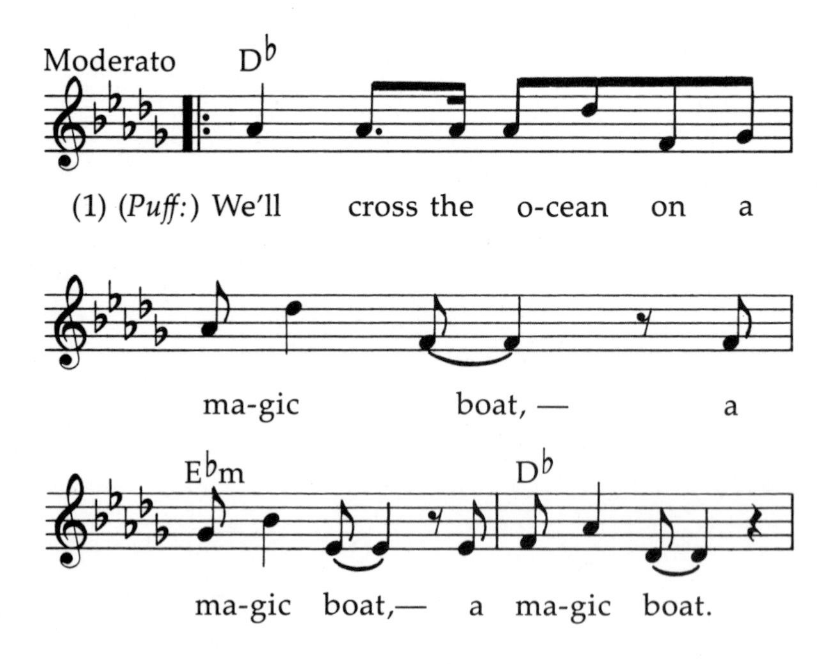

(Jackie:) Let's cross the o-cean on a
ma-gic boat (Both:) and
E♭m A♭ D♭ A♭
sail a - cross the wa-ter.
D♭
(Jackie:) Let's make the main - mast out of
E♭m
my bed- post,- my bed - post
D♭
my bed - post.

(Puff:) We'll make the main-mast out of
E♭m A♭
your bed - post (Both:) and sail a-cross the
D♭ B♭m
wa-ter. (Both:) When we get to a
Fm G♭
ma-gic land,- (Jackie:) Yes we can,- I
D♭ D♭7
know we can
G♭ Fm
(Both:) When we get to a ma-gic land

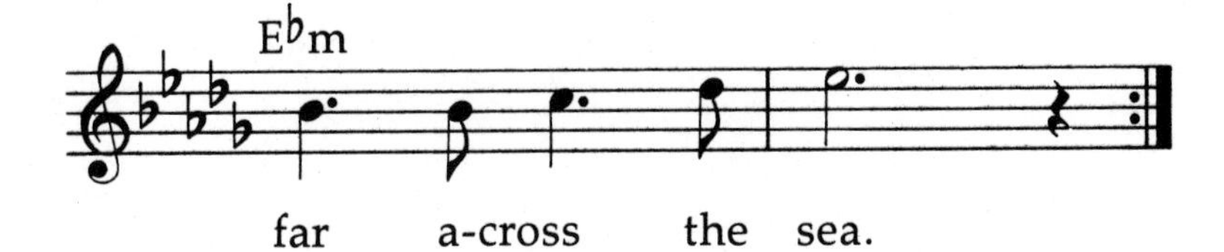

(2) (*Jackie*:) Let's make the rudder out of my guitar,
My guitar, my guitar.
(*Puff*:) We'll make the rudder out of your guitar
(*Both*:) And sail across the water.

(*Both*:) Now we can sail away to Hona-Lee,
Hona-Lee, Hona-Lee.
Now we can sail away to Hona-Lee
Far across the water.

(*Puff*:) Then you won't be frightened like you
were before . . .
[*abrupt fade*]

Weave Me the Sunshine

Words and music by Peter Yarrow

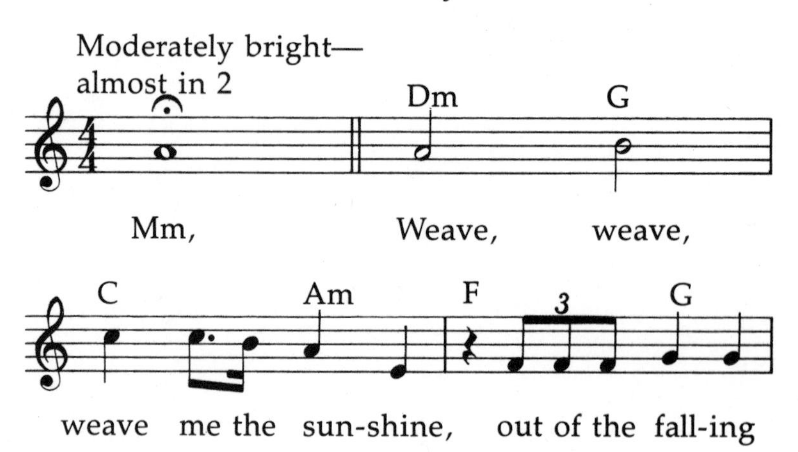

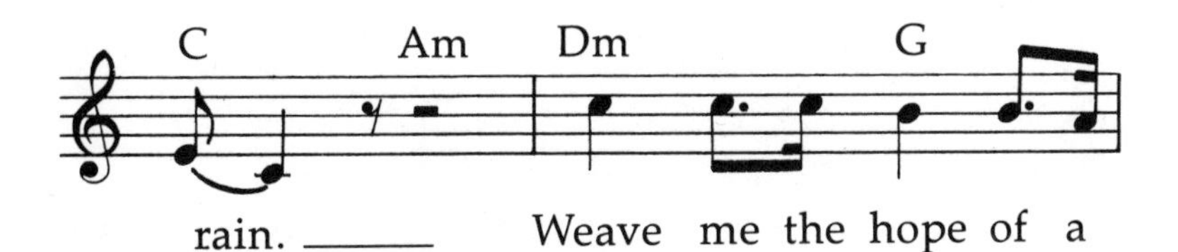

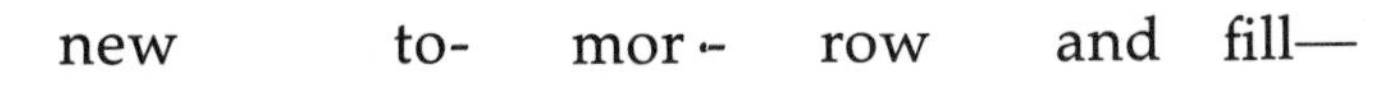

— my cup a- gain. ___ Sing it with me.

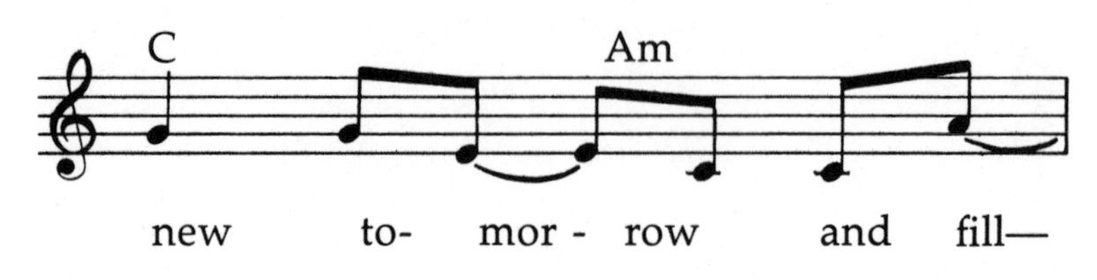

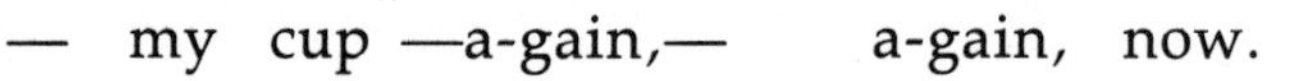

Weave, weave, weave me the sun-shine

out of the fall- ing rain.

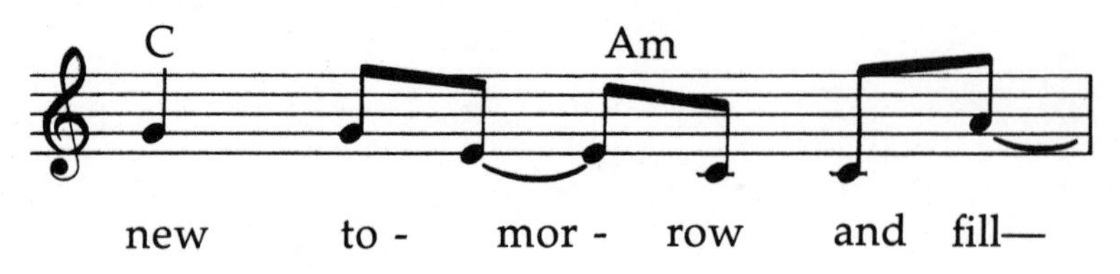

D
G
— my cup— a-gain.— Well, I've

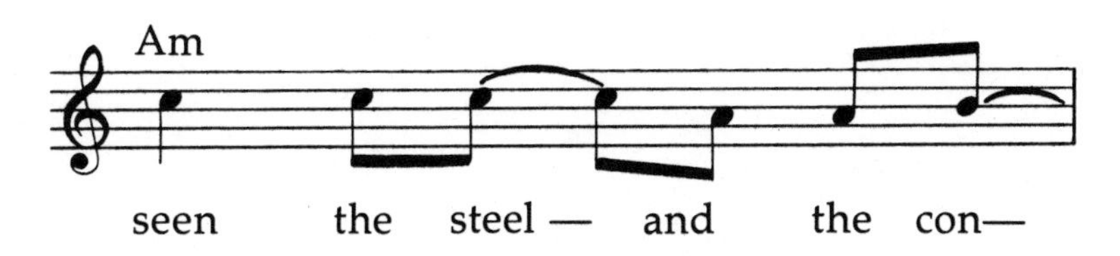
Am
seen the steel — and the con—

E
— crete crum - ble, —

F
G
C

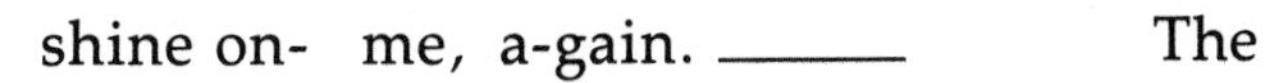
shine on- me, a-gain. ——— The

Am
D7
proud and the might-y, all have stum - bled,

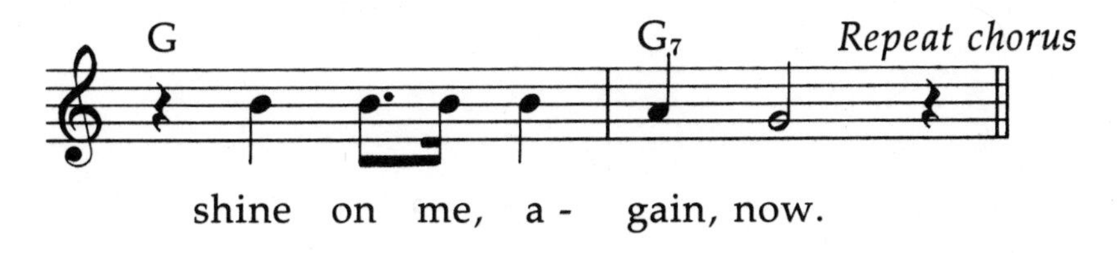
G
G7
Repeat chorus
shine on me, a - gain, now.

Am
E
They say that the tree of lov- - ing,
F
G
C
shine on me, a - gain, —
Am
grows on the bank of the
D_7
riv - er of suf - fer - ing,
G
G_7
Repeat chorus
shine on — me, a - gain. —
Am
E
If on-ly I — could heal— your sor - row,

F G C
shine — on me, a-gain, — I'd
Am D7
help you to find your new — to-mor-row,
G G Repeat chorus
shine on — me, a-gain. —
Am
Well, I've seen the steel — and the con —
E F G
— crete crum- ble, shine on me, a —
C Am
gain, — the proud and the might-y

D7
all got stum - bled,
G G7 Repeat chorus
shine on me, a- gain. —
Am E
On- ly you — can climb that moun -tain,
F G C
shine on me a - gain, If you —
Am D7
want to drink in the gold - en foun — tain,
Repeat chorus
twice to fade
G G7
shine — on me, a -gain, —sing it out, now.